NOT QUITE
BLACK
AND
WHITE

The artist used Adobe Photoshop to create the digital illustrations for this book.
Typography by Jeanne Hogle
16 17 18 19 20   SCP   10 9 8 7 6 5 4 3 2 1
❖
First Edition

NOT QUITE
BLACK AND WHITE

Written by Jonathan Ying
Illustrations by Victoria Ying

HARPER
An Imprint of HarperCollinsPublishers

Most zebras wear stripes,
but this one does not.

She much prefers dressing in PINK polka dot!

These penguins look dapper
in black and white suits.

But one funny fellow has
bright YELLOW boots!

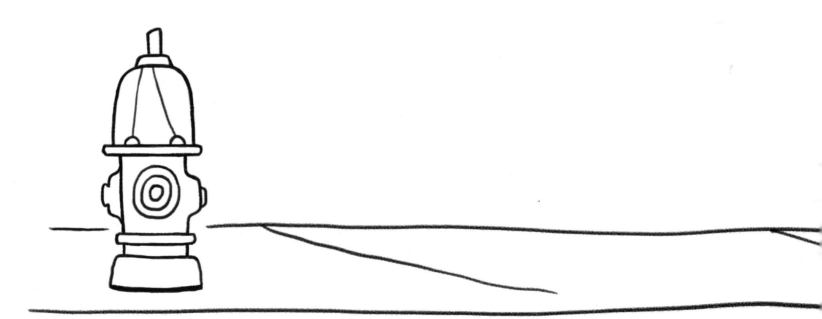

Dalmatians are sprinkled with spots of all shapes.

But some pups feel braver in flowing RED capes!

Look there! At the beach!
See two brother skunks!

They're easy to spot
in their matching BLUE trunks!

This llama likes climbing
up mountains and hills.

Her woolly BROWN scarf
keeps her safe from the chills.

This tiger is fancy,
the classiest cat—

from the tips of his toes
to his tall PURPLE hat!

This horse keeps the traffic under control.

His bright ORANGE vest shows he's on patrol!

This panda likes cooking
with sticks of bamboo.

His apron is messy
with leafy GREEN stew!

This cow rides a scooter to bring kids their milk.

She stays warm with a coat made from LAVENDER silk!

This kitty plays drums and he likes to rock.

He keeps the beat with his AQUA mohawk!

This badger goes on a trip to the moon.

The flag he will plant
is a striking MAROON!

We might have stripes, or we might have spots.

Sometimes we are fancy, sometimes we are not.

From the darkest of dark to the brightest of bright,

we're each pretty special, not quite **BLACK** and WHITE.